Y0-BDF-095

An Imprint of Sterling Publishing
387 Park Avenue South
New York, NY 10016

SANDY CREEK and the distinctive Sandy Creek logo are trademarks of Barnes and Noble, Inc.

© 2011 by Rockpool Children's Books Ltd.

This 2012 edition published by SANDY CREEK,
by arrangement with Rockpool Children's Books Ltd.

All rights reserved. No part of this publication may be reproduced,
stored in a retrieval system, or transmitted,
in any form or by any means, electronic, mechanical, photocopying,
recording, or otherwise, without prior written permission from the publisher.

Text and Illustrations © 2011 by Sam Walshaw
Sam Walshaw has asserted the moral rights
to be identified as the author and illustrator of this book.

ISBN 978-1-4351-3862-9

Printed in Singapore
Lot 2 4 6 8 10 9 7 5 3 1
IM JAN 2012 1

Sam Walshaw

Maisey and the
Pirates

Sandy Creek
NEW YORK

One day, Captain Codeye found an old treasure map.
"Aha!" he said, "'X' marks the spot where the sunken
treasure is!"

He told the pirate crew on the good ship Barnacle,
"It's a pirate's job to find hidden treasure.
We're setting sail for 'X' marks the spot!"

Soon Captain Codeye spied the 'X', and yelled,
"Drop the anchor, Crazy Maisey. We'll have to dive to the
bottom of the sea, to get to that sunken treasure."

"Aye, aye, Captain," shouted Maisey.

"Take a deep breath," gasped Crazy Maisey.

'SPLASH'
Captain Codeye
and Crazy Maisey
jumped in,

"There's the treasure!" gurgled Crazy Maisey.

"Fill your boots," bubbled Captain Codeye.
"Now head back up!"

Crazy Maisey and Captain Codeye
swam up towards the trusty Barnacle.
They couldn't wait to show
the treasure to the others,
but just as they were nearly there...

... they spotted a great big purple popeyed pirate-eating sea monster heading their way - and he looked very grumpy!

"Oh no! It's the purple, popeyed pirate-eating sea monster!" gurgled Captain Codeye, "QUICK!!!"

Captain Codeye and Crazy Maisey shot up out of the sea, and landed safely on the deck of the Barnacle.

"Phew! Hoist the sails!" shouted Captain Codeye. "It's the purple popeyed pirate-eating sea monster!"

Daisy quickly hoisted the sails.

But a few seconds later...
the purple popeyed pirate-eating sea
monster popped up, snarling and
waving his arms menacingly at them!

Everyone was too scared to do anything.

But then Daisy took charge –
even though she was the smallest of the pirates.
She stomped right up to the monster, and told him
off for being such a mean, grumpy bully!

The purple popeyed pirate-eating
sea monster was so shocked
that he burst into tears.

"There, there" said Daisy.
She handed the monster a tissue
and invited him on to the Barnacle
for yummy cakes –
as long as he behaved himself.

The monster was shy at first, but he felt better when he had a piece of cake, and they saw he really was quite a nice monster after all!

The monster said he was sorry for being so
mean and grumpy. "I've got this terrible itch
on my back. It's made me meaner and meaner,
and grumpier and grumpier," he explained.

Daisy had a look and squeaked, "Blistering barnacles!
There's an octopus stuck down your pants!
His tentacles must have been tickling you all this time!
I'll pull him out."

"Aaaaaahhhhh!" At last the itch had gone. The monster felt so much better, he promised not to scare anyone again - at least not on purpose! "By the way," he said, "I don't really eat pirates. I'd much rather have a nice cupcake."

The monster thanked the crew of the good ship Barnacle and went on his way. He was a much happier monster now that he'd got rid of that itch...and the octopus is happy to be out of his pants too!